THE
PIANO MAN'S
CHRISTMAS

THE
PIANO MAN'S
CHRISTMAS

And Other Stories
for Christmas

Ira Williams, Jr.

Abingdon Press

Nashville

The Piano Man's Christmas:
And Other Stories for Christmas

Copyright © 1986 by Abingdon Press

This book is printed on acid-free paper.

Library of Congress Cataloging-in-Publication Data

WILLIAMS, IRA E., 1926
  The piano man's Christmas
and other stories for Christmas.
  1. Christmas stories. I. Title.
  PS3573.I44927P5   1986   813'.54   86-3527

ISBN 0-687-30920-4 (alk. paper)

MANUFACTURED BY THE PARTHENON PRESS AT
NASHVILLE, TENNESSEE, UNITED STATES OF AMERICA

To my parents,
Ira and Carolyn McLeod Williams,
who first taught me the songs of Christmas—
and why we sing them

Contents

Preface

Jesus said, "If I be lifted up, I will draw all men unto me." Those words continue to ring true in our human experience. Christ is ever our contemporary, his appeal so universal no race or nation can claim him as an exclusive possession, yet his great heart of love makes him one with all peoples.

These five Christmas stories are offered as an expression of the continuing power of the Incarnation. They have been written to express a kinship with Christians of the Native American, Asian, Black, Anglo-American, and Hispanic cultures. They have grown out of my personal contact with people from varied ethnic communities whose faith has enriched my own. The language forms are those with which my friends in other cultures have most freely spoken their faith to me. The stories are fiction, but the experiences they convey are real. Each has its special source of inspiration.

For fourteen years I served as a pastor in New Mexico. Many small isolated villages there have kept a link with their past, which the modern world has only recently begun to erase. "Christmas at Cañon Belen" was inspired by the discovery of one such village near our mountain cabin.

My boyhood years were spent in southern Mississippi. New Orleans was our shopping center, so that city has always brought back warm memories. A special treasure of those years was a fascination with the wit and wisdom of elderly friends I came to know in the Black culture. The memory of their creativity still inspires me, and I find that same gift today in many of my Black colleagues in ministry—Zan Holmes and Bishops Leontine Kelly, W. T. Handy, and Ernest Dixon. "The Piano Man's Christmas" is a tribute to the spirit of such men and women I remember from my youth.

Born into the home of a pastor, my brothers and I knew something of the proverbial fishbowl in which "preacher's kids" live out their lives. My mother, also a preacher's child, recalled for us the even more rigid life-style of her teenage years in the parsonage. "The Tumbleweed Christmas of 1920" shares some of those joys and struggles, although the setting has been changed to the high plains of West Texas, my present home.

The appeal of China has its roots in the visits of missionaries to our home when I was a child. The opportunity for travel to mainland China in 1982 brought back special memories of places I had heard described almost fifty years earlier, as well as the spirit of the Chinese Christians praised by those missionaries. "The Humiliation of Li Huan Liu" is a tribute to the faithful Christians who kept the church alive in their hearts and homes during the difficult years of the "cultural revolution." A newer constitution now permits freedom of religion in China.

My first visit to the Navajo reservation took place at mid-century, before the pick-up truck had replaced the horse and many of the blessings and curses of the 1980s had made their impact on the life of Native Americans in the remote areas of northern New Mexico and Arizona. "For Love of a Horse" recalls the beautiful spirit of the Navajo friends I met in those years.

None of the stories is intended as a yearning for "the good old days," or as a wish for a more primitive life-style for any ethnic group. The tales are, rather, a tribute to the spirit of my friends, at the time I came to know them, in the situation in which I met them. They are, above all, a witness to the love of Christ, which transcends all times and cultures and barriers of race and color.

A special word of thanks is due the following persons who had a part in the preparation and evaluation of the stories: my wife, Marilyn, who read and reread the stories with me; Dot Clark, who helped type the material; and Leontine Kelly, for her evaluation and commendation of the manuscript. I also wish to thank the people who read individual stories and made helpful suggestions related to the various ethnic cultures: Sister Janie Briseño of the Roman Catholic diocesan office in Amarillo; the Reverend William Williams, a United Methodist pastor in Amarillo; Dr. Kenneth McIntosh, former missionary to Hong Kong and a staff member of the Board of Global Ministries; Dr. Tom Cloyd, council director for the Tennessee Conference and former superintendent of the Navajo Methodist Mission School in Farmington, New Mexico; and the Reverend Fred Yazzie, an ordained United Methodist Navajo pastor of Shiprock, New Mexico. Thanks, too, to my children and grandchildren, who pleaded repeatedly, "Papa, tell us a story."

Christmas
at Cañon Belen

Maria Gonzales turned away from the outdoor oven and brushed her floury palms on the apron around her ample waist. She sat to rest on a crumbling rock wall and looked out over the sweep of her world, which spread from the mountain crest to the church courtyard in the valley below. The laughter of children at play echoed up the canyon walls. She watched them crack the whip and spin the younger tots off one by one, sprawling—and sometimes bawling.

Her eyes searched out one small boy who had broken his link in the weaving human chain and dropped exhausted on the steps of the church—one more sign to trouble the woman's mind. She had never seen Pablo drop out of a game till the last child had given up, but these last few weeks he seemed to tire so easily.

The distant whine of an engine interrupted her thoughts. She looked up toward the mountain pass where a chartreuse panel truck was raising dust on the old logging road. Suddenly the driver hit the brakes and turned abruptly down the switchback trail that ended at Cañon Belen.* She wondered what could bring the gaudy van to their little village. The mixed blessings of civilization had not yet reached this tiny spot in the pine forest. No electric wires swept the sky. No telephone booth stood at the bend in the road. Not even a gas station or minimarket was to be found. Few maps even carried the name of this small settlement untouched by the changing times. Why were strangers descending into their tranquil valley?

Maria walked to the porch of her ancestral home to get a better view of the approaching truck. The squat adobe house

*Spanish for *Bethlehem Canyon.*

stood in a row of small dwellings which had weathered the elements of more than three centuries since the forebears of this sturdy stock of mountain people first came from the Old World. Still the men clung to the land, following their herds of sheep and cattle and tilling the rock-strewn hillside. Their only touch with the outside world was the lumbering yellow bus that took their children to the nearest mission school, rare stops by the United States mail car, and a weekly visit by the priest to hold Mass at the chapel of Our Lady of Guadalupe.

The truck coasted into the village square, and the old woman squinted into the sun as she saw the driver pull to a stop in front of the weathered church. A tall man eased from the driver's seat and unfolded his gaunt frame. A short, stocky companion seemed to bounce from the other door. One of the men walked over to Pablo and squatted beside him on the steps of the church. Soon the boy was looking up and pointing toward the cottage where Maria was standing. She watched as they began to climb the steep hillside, the tall man following Pablo easily while his fat little friend puffed sluggishly behind.

"Ma-ma!" the boy shouted, running ahead of them to the house. "This is Pete and that's Mike! They want to talk to you."

Señora Gonzales pulled the faded shawl more tightly about her shoulders. Many winters in the mountain snows had joined with personal tragedy to carve deep lines in her face. She searched the eyes of the two men with an ageless wisdom, and her words were guarded as she greeted them with an enthusiasm somewhat less exuberant than that of the boy.

"Pablo says you've come to talk to me. What do you want of the people in Cañon Belen? The rest of the world has passed us by. Why do you come here?"

The lean man stepped forward. "My name's Pete Johnson, Señora. I'm a writer, and my partner, Mike Blodgett, is a photographer for *Pioneer Magazine.*"

The old woman's eyes flashed. "That's what I thought! You're here to take our pictures and spread them around where your kind of people can laugh at us—how ignorant and backward we are. Get out! Now!"

The man named Pete kept shaking his head. "No, Señora Gonzales! No! You don't understand. Let me explain."

"Don't explain anything. Just leave us alone!" she cut in with instinctive suspicion.

The man put his hand on Pablo's shoulder and said, "Please hear me out. My editors believe America has forgotten some of its most beautiful past—the first pioneers. Most people know about the Pilgrims and the Mayflower. But not many school children know of the settlers who came to this country long before the Pilgrims touched New England. They see the Spanish only as fortune hunters who sailed to the New World and went back to Spain disappointed."

"We know better, don't we, Ma-ma?" Pablo broke in, and the woman nodded.

"Yes, *you* know," Pete agreed, "but most Americans have forgotten the Castilian colonists who came to New Mexico to make a home in the wilderness. My magazine believes that people like you can help us learn their story. Won't you work with us, Señora?"

Maria Gonzales looked out beyond the mountaintops, but she was thinking back across the years.

"All we remember is what our parents passed down to us. There's not much to tell. No one cares today how many sheep and pans and spoons old Manuel Ornelas brought along when he marched with Coronado."

"You're wrong!" Pete pleaded. "This is a new generation,

17

Señora. Some of us care much more than you think. Share your story with us."

"Come in," she invited. "We must talk some more." She poured coffee for the men and Pablo sprawled on a sheepskin rug as the two strangers unfolded their plan. They wanted to interview the families in Cañon Belen who might have a link with the past. Perhaps some of them had kept heirlooms, handed down from one generation to the next, which they could photograph. The men would need the help of Señora Gonzales to open doors for them, and Pablo could be their assistant. The tall stranger reached for his billfold and offered a fifty-dollar bill to the old woman as an advance payment for her services.

The proud matriarch shook her head with an offended dignity. "Keep your money, Señor. My friends and I—we are not for sale. Our story is sacred to us. We have kept it in our hearts these many years. I am sure that is where it belongs. I don't think we want to peddle our family secrets to a gawking world."

"But Señora Gonzales, your people have helped to make America—just as the Anglo did. It's a wonderful story. Think of Pablo and the other children. Not all of them will stay in your hidden valley. Some will go out into a world where they will need encouragement to hold their heads high. You can do that by telling us your story. So can your friends."

"Let me think tonight," she said. "You come back tomorrow."

She knew the men were disappointed, but Maria needed time. If they really wanted her story, they could wait another day. Besides, a special blessing of her people was their unhurried confidence in the wisdom of mañana—lesson one for the strangers!

She watched from the window as the men walked down the hill, Pablo at their side. They reached the truck, and she could see the man named Pete slip folding money into Pablo's hand.

"The rascal," she murmured, "so he thinks he'll reach me through the boy. What kind of fool does he think I am? He should know a small boy can't hide money from his Mama."

But she knew Pete was also a smart customer. She would do anything for Pablo, and the man had been sharp enough to note her doting manner. She still carried the burden of her daughter's death from the strange sickness that had swept through their valley. It had come so soon after the stroke that took Papa Gonzales; and now this grandson was all she had to live for. Yes, if they were good to Pablo, she might yet tell them her story.

The morning sun had barely filled the floor of the canyon when the garish truck rolled once more into the courtyard of the mission church. Maria Gonzales watched an excited Pablo greet his new friends and lead them once more up the mountain path. She opened the door and welcomed them to a warm room where a spotless cloth covered the heavy oak table. A loaf of fresh-baked bread flooded the room with its fragrance; beside it on the table sat a dish of prickly-pear jelly and a mound of butter molded with an artist's touch—all signs that the coldness of their reception the night before had been thawed by a little boy's diplomacy. Pablo pulled sturdy hide-woven chairs to the table and offered them to his friends. The grandmother lifted a pot from the ancient hearth in the corner and poured steaming cups of black coffee.

Then she sat down and told the story of her family—the ancestor who had fought alongside Coronado and returned to this land with a bride and their few treasures. Most of the wares he brought from the old country had worn out or been discarded long ago. She hesitated, then, suppressing a grin, pushed away from the table and waddled across the room.

From a small cabinet above the rough-hewn bedstead in the corner, she drew out a golden goblet and placed it lovingly on the table.

"It was a gift to my great-great-grandfather from the Duke of Albuquerque. The Bishop has blessed it so the padrecito can use it for the Mass of the Nativity." She beamed as the small man took his camera and photographed the glistening vessel—one last fragment of something precious from her past.

"But come," she said, "we must go now." She lifted the treasure back to its place of honor, then led the men through the door and along the trail. In the days that followed, she introduced them to her friends in the canyon, and Pete scribbled notes on each family's history while Mike took pictures of the relics from the past. They discovered a priceless Madonna in the home of Carmen Garcia, and a primitive painting, probably worth a small fortune, had been handed down to Ruben Gutierrez. Sterling silver that once belonged to the king of Spain lay stashed in the closet of Juan Martinez. A small ebony chest with precious stones that had been worn by a duchess was all the pride and dignity left for Christina Sandoval.

Maria was delighted to see the astonishment on the faces of the two men at the value of these antique treasures from their past. But she was thrilled also to know that her friends shared the excitement each time the strangers took pictures and showed a sample of the magazine that would carry their story.

She would say, "Imagine, Carmen! You and Juan on a magazine cover. We will make our children proud of their mamas and papas."

"Think of it, Ruben. They're going to tell your story to the whole world."

"How about that, Christina? Nice picture."

And everyone would nod and smile, "Si, Si!"

Señora Gonzales was aglow at the thought of sharing their heritage with the outside world, and with Pablo so happy, all her cares were forgotten.

The good people in Cañon Belen became so engrossed in the project that when the holiest day of their year had arrived they were not prepared. The village patriarch recalled that it was the day before Christmas—the manger scene had yet to be built in the church for midnight Mass, and there was much cooking still to be done. Maria invited the two strangers to stay for the great event and they accepted gladly, for this too was a part of the Castilian past. No one would dare to miss the Mass of the Nativity and the joyful celebration that would follow. She suggested that the men park their truck on a little rise above the square where they could watch the candlelight procession before the Mass. Then she joined the rest of the villagers in the hurried preparations for the holy night.

As the shadows of the afternoon lengthened, Maria saw the Padre arrive and make his way to the adobe mission at the center of the village. She was startled to hear him toll the ancient bell until the deep bass tones had summoned every family in the valley. It was hours before the service—why would the priest steal precious moments from their last-minute chores on Christmas Eve? They all hurried to the steps of the church, wondering what surprise he had in store for them. Everyone was present but the two strangers. Maria made a mental note to go and tell them what it was all about when the priest finished.

She heard the Father call Pablo. "In my car there are candles for the Christmas Mass. Will you get them for me and help me in the chapel? I will be there very soon. Wait for me at the altar."

Señora Gonzales watched the boy scamper away, but her face fell as the priest called her. He put his arm around her shoulder, and she trembled at the burden of sadness in his eyes. He turned to the villagers.

"My friends, you remember that last week I took our Pablo to the doctor. The report on his tests has come back. It is a rare kind of sickness. I must take him to a hospital in the city beyond the mountains. It will cost many dollars to make him well, so when you come to the chapel tonight—the offering we bring for the sake of the Christ Child—it will help to heal our Pablo. But for now, let us make this night a very happy time for him."

The desolate grandmother watched the families move away slowly to their homes on the hillside. It was the season to be joyful, but the words of the priest had come like a knife to kill their laughter. This village was so like a family that any sorrow that touched one reached the hearts of all. Quietly, more reverently than ever before, the people made their preparations for the midnight service in the chapel.

The tearful woman remembered the strangers and their friendship with Pablo. They, too, would want to know the doctor's verdict. She walked along the rock-strewn roadway to share with them the common sorrow of the village. As she approached the truck, the woman could not believe the words she heard. Crouching near the window, she could see an amused smirk on the face of the thin man.

"This has been the easiest job we ever tackled, Mike. These gullible old fools—to think that any editor would buy this kind of drivel."

"That's a laugh all right. But the treasures—they're real enough. What do you think we can get for all that loot?"

"I figure it ought to be worth at least twenty thousand. That's not bad for a week's work."

"But we still have to lift the stuff. Can we make it?"

"Don't get edgy, Mike. This whole canyon will be at midnight Mass. They leave everything out in the open. I could find their treasures in the dark. In a half-hour we can take all that's worth selling and be gone. Don't worry."

The old woman, enraged, turned to storm down the hill toward the chapel, but the license plate at the back of the truck snagged her apron. The sound roused the two men and they bolted from the cab. Wrestling her to the ground, they stifled her anguished cries for help, gagged her, and bound her hands and feet. Then they shoved her rudely into the front seat of the truck, and there she waited helplessly until the bell in the steeple rang once more, calling the people to Christmas Eve Mass.

The sky was a dazzling ocean of stars, but it brought no calm to the troubled woman. Hot tears rolled down her face as she watched the procession wind its way toward the centuries-old church. When the last silent figure had moved through the doors, she saw the sinister forms of the two strangers slip away toward the homes in the settlement to carry out their plot.

Maria Gonzales had scanned every inch of her cramped prison, seeking some means of escape. A triumphant smile crossed her lips as her captors disappeared on the darkened trail. The men had been careless enough to overlook a broken splinter of glass in the side window of the truck. The determined woman stretched her puffy wrists against the sharp edge. Moving the twisted ropes up and down, she could feel the fibers giving way until her hands were free. The knotted cords that tied her aching ankles resisted more stubbornly, but she would not give up until she could pull one foot, then the other, from her loosened fetters. She thrust the door open and, running and panting and stumbling in the dark, rushed down the mountainside toward the church.

She burst into the mission just as the priest had come to the close of his Christmas message and was moving toward the altar. The beauty of the scene overwhelmed the weary woman. A small pump organ filled the chapel with the strains of an old Spanish carol. Never was the bread and wine brought to the Padre with more loving hands than through the ministrations of young Pablo, who seemed to hover above the crèche like a member of the angelic host. Quick tears welled in her eyes as she caught a glimpse of the gifts to the Christ Child—a priceless Madonna, an antique painting, sterling silver that bore a king's insignia, a small ebony chest of precious stones.

Only a Father God could know the love these sturdy mountain people felt for one another that brought them to part with such treasures . . . and only God—and Mama Gonzales—knew why two bewildered men drove away in a chartreuse panel truck, cursing the village and its people.

The
Piano Man's
Christmas

The old piano man ran his fingers up and down the keys in a blues tune and sang a few sad notes to himself. It was Christmas Eve and business had been slow all afternoon. A lone straggler put his glass down on the bar and waved a half-hearted good-bye to the manager. A melancholy calm settled over the room. Amos let the number fade off into a soft, heart-breaking minor key and looked back over his shoulder to see if anyone were still around.

"Go ahead and take off, Amos," the owner mumbled through his cigar. "You're making me homesick with that blues stuff, and I don't even have a family to go home to. We'll close up tomorrow. I'll see you the day after. Merry Christmas!"

"Same to you," the old man answered, but his heart wasn't in it. He picked up a half-empty bottle of gin from behind the bar and slipped out into the night. "Homesick and nobody to go home to! Boss man's a lot like me. Merrrry Christmas," he scowled. "One whole day to get away from it all. For this old Black piano man, there ain't much to run away from, and nothing to run away to."

He took a deep drink from the bottle and his memories were as bitter as the gin. It hurt to think about it, but some things the old head won't let you forget. He had met a good woman one summer in Mobile. "Lord, she was a beauty." He had played jazz in a little restaurant just off Government Street, and they had put her on one day as a waitress—Dinah Lee. She could glide between those tables with a six-service tray balanced on her shoulder as graceful as a ballet dancer, and never spill a drop of gumbo or forget an order. He had walked her home one night, and before the frost nipped the tender buds on the autumn rose they were man and wife.

Then he got a piano job at the Admiral Semmes Hotel. Young Amos was moving up in the world. That was real fine, because a special mothering look started showing up in Dinah's eyes. Already he could see every dollar of his raise spent to outfit a nursery. Amos became the proudest papa in all Mobile when he looked into the face of their baby girl.

"She's an angel, Dinah. That's going to be her name. Angel." He lifted the infant in his arms and strutted around the room. "Angel, I'm going to write you the prettiest song any piano man ever played. You just see if I don't." They didn't have to promise him heaven after death. Heaven had already arrived.

The old man shuffled on down Bourbon Street and took another deep drink from the bottle. "Only trouble with a young man, he never knows how to hold on to a good thing when he's got it."

All the folks at the Admiral Semmes had started taking to the new jazz tunes like crazy. Some of the visiting big shots from New York heard him play one night and planted the dream of Broadway's bright lights in the star-struck little ivory tickler. And somewhere along the way, between the dizzy success that made his head too big for his hat and the chorus girls that sat on his piano and tickled his chin, Dinah and the little girl had slipped out of his life.

The man turned down a side street. A puff of wind blew the clutter of the pavement past his shuffling feet. The damp chill of winter on the Mississippi seemed to reach all the way to his bones while the gin did its work. What does an old piano man have to live for when arthritis slows down his fingers, and his bones ache, and he's lost the only two people who ever really loved him, and there's nothing to go home to but an empty room?

He stepped over the puddle of tepid waste in the alley and walked under the soft lights over the pawn shop window. The coal stove at the back of the store looked inviting and he eased his way through the door and down the narrow aisle to the glowing heater. While he rubbed his hands, he couldn't miss the counter beside him. Every variety of hand gun you could ask for was laid out under the glass, from dull Saturday-night specials to the spit-and-polish brand names used by the professionals. When Amos left the shop, a small gun nestled in the pocket of his woolen jacket. One little bullet to the temple and it would be over—the pain, the loneliness, the bitter memories. He headed toward his drab flat with a quickened pace.

The piano man came to Canal Street and turned toward the shopping district. A small Black girl stood in front of the big department store, wide-eyed at the window display of the Christmas story. The decorators had spared no expense in creating the tableau—a marble-pillared inn, an immaculate manger made of finished hardwoods, a crib of solid polished mahogany. The Baby Jesus was an endearing cherub with blond curls. All the biblical figures were elegant white ladies and gentlemen, robed in silks and velvet, every hair on their heads, even the flowing beards, combed and perfectly in place.

Amos watched the child as she stood on tiptoe and pressed her little nose against the glass that separated her from the holy family. A uniformed doorman for the exclusive store had been glaring at the girl from the time she had stopped to adore the figures in the window. He rushed up, grabbed the frail shoulders, and jerked her around.

"Get your nose off that window, kid. If I catch you rubbing your greasy face on that glass again, you're going to get what's coming to you."

The piano man ran to the window and pulled the child from the doorman's rough grip.

"Take your grubby hands off her. A big strong man like you must be real proud of himself. Not just anybody can make a little girl cry. Look at her, scared out of her wits."

"Don't you trifle with me, old man. Get her out of here."

Amos lifted the child gently in his arms and walked past the store, but not in time to spare her the insults of the man behind them: "Little Black rascals are always messing up something."

The old man hugged her close. "Honey, don't you pay no attention to him. He's poor white trash."

His words brought little consolation to the sobbing child. She kept insisting, "I just wanted to see the baby."

"I know that, honey."

"But I just wanted to see the baby."

"I know you did," he tried to comfort her.

She could say only, "I just wanted to see the baby."

"Don't you worry, now. Don't fret that pretty little head no more." He looked into her eyes and promised, "I'm going to show you the Baby Jesus; but we got to wipe away those tears first. You wouldn't want Baby Jesus to see you crying, would you?"

"No," she sniffed and rubbed her eyes.

"No, I didn't think so." Amos shook his head. "Now, what's your name, honey?"

"Angel," she whispered.

Just the sound of the name gave him pain. And the memory of a long-lost face brought tears he tried to brush away before the child could see them.

He forced himself to say, "Angel, honey, I want to tell you something. That Baby Jesus in the window, and the mother, and the shepherds. That's not the way they looked. Let me show you how it really was. Let's go in here."

He shoved open the door to Woolworth's and took the child to the toy section. In one corner at the back of the store, he reached up on a top shelf and pulled down a doll. The face was chocolate brown, and there were little black ringlets on the boy-doll's head, and thick little lips that curled into a smile.

"Now you come with me, Angel, and I'll show you how it really was the night Baby Jesus was born."

He paid for the doll and led the child by the hand to the next corner, where they turned and walked back toward old New Orleans. Friends waved to the piano man as he came to a small hotel that had seen better times. Loose mortar had allowed many of the bricks to fall out, leaving jagged holes along the facade. Most of the paint had flaked off the sign long ago, so only the regular tenants of the area any longer knew the name of the place. The soiled windowpane revealed a cramped lobby containing only a plain desk, a battered upright piano, and two horsehair couches with cracks in the imitation leather where some of the stuffing was bulging out. A stained drab-green awning, half its tassels gone, hung over the window.

"How you doing, Joseph?" the old man called to the shoeshine boy on the corner.

"I'm doing fine, Mr. Amos. Just getting ready to put everything away for the night."

"Don't go away yet, Joseph. I need you to help me with something." Then, "Hey, Ruby," he yelled through the door of the hotel. "Anybody here?"

"On the way," a voice echoed down the hall from behind a bundle of soiled sheets and bedspreads. A young woman walked into the lobby, dropped the laundry in a corner, and smiled. "Come on in, Mr. Piano Man, and play me a tune. I'm ready for a good blues song."

"Maybe later, but right now I need you to do something for me. Ruby, this is Angel, and I want you to help me tell her all about the first Christmas."

"Me? What do I know about the first Christmas?"

"You just do like I tell you. Hey, Joseph, let me have that shoeshine stool. Now let's put it right here under that awning.

Ruby, you sit here on the stool, and Joseph, you stand there by Ruby, kinda like you're protecting her. Now, Angel, we'll let Ruby borrow your doll for a little bit. Okay, honey?" The child gave up her new toy reluctantly, and Amos placed the boy-doll carefully in the crook of the hotel maid's arm.

"Now, Angel," he began, "when the Baby Jesus was born, it wasn't in front of a great big inn with marble columns. And the crib wasn't sitting under a polished mahogany stable. It was in front of a crumbling-down hotel, and the stable wasn't much different from this old streaky awning hanging out over the sidewalk."

He walked to the pile of laundry and pulled out two sheets. A white one, which wasn't very soiled, was placed around Ruby's shoulders, and he draped a brown-stained one on Joseph. "And they weren't wearing silks and velvets, Angel. Mary and Joseph had on plain old cotton clothes like you and me wear."

The surprise tableau on the corner had begun to attract the attention of people going home from the little shops, but the old man was oblivious to their presence. "And another thing, Angel. That little family in the stable didn't have snow-white faces, and the Baby Jesus wasn't a blue-eyed blond. His skin was olive brown, and he had little black curls all over the top of his head. And Joseph was as dark as me, from building houses out in the sun. And the mother, Mary—she was a pretty little dark girl, about the color of Ruby here."

He looked up at the bystanders forming a semicircle around them and recognized an old friend. "Hey, come here, Billy." He stood the man on the left of the two figures under the awning. "Oh, and you too, Tony. You kneel over here on the left. Here, Billy, you take this walking cane and hold it in your hand. It makes a pretty good shepherd's crook." Then he placed threadbare blankets around each of the two men.

"Now, Angel," he turned to the girl, "Billy here works out at the stockyard, and Tony unloads cargo on the docks. They're not shepherds, but they work as hard as the shepherds did, and they both handle sheep. And they both get wore out and almost give up sometimes, like the Bible shepherds did; and they need some good tidings just like the old-timey men did."

The gathering crowd was catching the mood of the old man's drama, and one young girl started singing just above a whisper, "Go Tell It on the Mountain." Soon everybody was singing and swaying while Amos talked.

"Come here, Jesse," he called to a man so feeble he could hardly shuffle. "You stand over there on the other side, just at the edge of the awning." He turned back to the child. "Now, honey, old Jesse here's been through a lot. When he was a young man he got mis-accused and whipped with a rope and hung up to die, only his woman cut him down and he didn't die. He's seen a heap of things happen, and he knows how sweet it is just to be alive. He's a wise man. That's the kind of folks that came from the East bringing gifts to the Baby Jesus."

He finished forming a turban around the old man's head with a bright-colored towel and reached into the crowd for a tall young fellow. "Come here, Mac. Let me put this robe on you." He pulled out a big blue spread from the laundry pile and draped the man's shoulders, then topped his head with another towel. "You stand over there, Mac, right next to Jesse; only I want you bending over and looking at the baby." The young man dutifully obliged.

"Now, Angel, you take Mac here. He's a tall handsome man. He had a wife and a beautiful little girl, just like you, honey. And everybody here knows he got to fooling around with the bottle and chasing women, and his woman picked up his little baby and went away. Then Mac, he made a turn-around, and he went and begged her to come back home. She finally did, and Mac, here, he's got his life all straightened back up again. That's a wise man, Angel. That's what the Bible story means by wise men. It's not silk and velvet clothes that makes a man wise. It's getting smart like Jesse and Mac that makes a wise man."

The distant whine of a patrol car sounded down the street. The siren grew in intensity, but the old man was too engrossed to notice until a giant-sized police officer rolled out of the car's door and roared, "What's going on here? Break it up, folks. Christmas Eve wasn't meant for street fighting."

He pushed his way through the crowd, then caught his breath at the figures under the awning. The Black patrolman took off his hat and mumbled apologies to the old piano man, who continued to talk to the little girl as if nothing had happened.

"That's the way it really was, Angel. The manger folks were just like these friends of mine and yours, here on the sidewalk."

The child walked over to the figures in the live tableau beneath the awning, while the crowd picked up the strains of "Silent Night, Holy Night." She looked up at the wise men, then walked over to the shepherds. Finally coming to the holy family, she ran her fingers through the curly black hair of the doll in Ruby's arms, then stood before them all in pure rapture. She came back to the old man and turned again to take in the whole scene.

"Angel," Amos whispered, "the Baby Jesus is one of us. Don't you ever let anybody make you feel different, honey. He walked the same kind of road we walk. He knew what it was to be made fun of and to be hurt and to be treated like he was dirt under the feet of the big folks in the city. But God took care of that. From now on, honey, wherever you go, you just remember he's walking right there with you, and there ain't nothing the two of you can't handle."

Suddenly the big Black policeman started singing "Sweet Little Jesus Boy," and up and down the street other singers echoed the refrain, "Sweet little Holy Child, we didn't know 'twas you." It was as if time had rolled back and the streets of New Orleans had become the cobblestone village of Bethlehem.

After a while the old man said to the child, "Angel, honey, your mama's going to be worried about you. Can I walk you home?"

"Let me," the patrolman volunteered, and Amos caught the wide-eyed wonder on the child's face at so many surprises in one night. Ruby handed Amos the boy-doll, and he bent over to place it in Angel's arms. She reached for the old man and hugged him as tight as her small arms could squeeze. Then she kissed his cheek and said, "I love you, Mr. Piano Man."

He watched her drive away in the patrol car, the siren going full force. When he turned back to the tableau, the crowd had dispersed into the night, and his friends were handing the sheets and towels and blankets back to Ruby.

"Thank you," Amos said. A kind of reverence that made speech seem out of place still hung in the air, and they only gripped his hand and patted him on the shoulder and went their separate ways.

The piano man stood alone under the awning. For the first time, Amos himself had really seen Christmas. He slipped the gun from his pocket, dropped it down the sewer grating at the curb, and made his way home, fingering on an imaginary keyboard the notes to "Sweet Little Jesus Boy."

The
Tumbleweed
Christmas of
1920

"Now you listen to me, Sam Ogletree! You're not going to sashay off to some protracted meeting in Amarillo the week before Christmas. You're going to be right here in Prairie City on Christmas Eve, doing a little pastoral care for your own family."

"But, Sarah," the man protested, "this is the opportunity of a lifetime."

"Don't you 'but Sarah' me. And wipe that pious-martyr look off your face. This is one time your family needs you a lot more than the 'sinner folks' in Amarillo do."

"Sarah, you've got to be reasonable. I've been asked to take a prominent part in the closing rally of the Foursquare Gospel crusade. That's a mighty big honor!"

"Honor my foot! *Temptation* is more like it. There's plenty of men besides Sam Ogletree that Aimee Semple McPherson* can flatter into saying a prayer at her revival meeting. She *would* end her crusade on the Sunday night before Christmas Eve, the time when men belong at home with their wives and children. By the time you ride that old horse of yours from Amarillo back to Prairie City, Christmas will have come and gone. If you don't have the gumption to write Sister Aimee and say no, then I'll just sit down and do it for you." She slammed the bathroom door so soundly the Reverend Olgetree misdirected a swipe with his razor and nicked the end of his nose.

Brother Sam, as his congregation affectionately spoke of him, knew this was not the appropriate time to press the matter. Sarah allowed him to be the head of his household in

*A popular evangelist of the era and founder of the International Church of the Foursquare Gospel.

public, and even brag about it from the pulpit. She also expected him to discipline the children and to be the breadwinner. He had learned to his dismay, however, that when certain boundaries were crossed and her temper flared, he dared not push his luck. There was no question that this was one of those times.

He applied a touch of alum to the nick on his nose, finished shaving, and prepared himself for breakfast. The children were waiting when he walked into the dining room.

"Good morning, David. Good morning, Rachel. Good morning, Matthew. And good morning, my little Rebekah." He addressed them in the descending order of their ages.

"Good morning, Papa," the children dutifully answered, as one voice.

"I see your mother has prepared a real feast. Well, what are we waiting for?" They sat down at the groaning table and he turned to the oldest. "David, will you say grace for us?"

"It's Rachel's turn!"

"No, it's not! I had to say it last night!"

Under Reverend Ogletree's withering look, his son grudgingly said "Lord bless this food to our bodies and our souls to thy service Amen" so hastily that Rebekah didn't have time to close her eyes, nor Matthew to pop the biggest sausage into his mouth unseen. The parson had a mind to ask the boy to repeat the prayer more reverently, but his own position this morning was so precarious, he chose to let the meal move along as quickly and quietly as possible and make an early escape to the seclusion of his study. Alas, he was not spared that privilege.

Rebekah won a race with Matthew to see who could eat fastest, then turned her attention to more important matters. "Papa, you *are* coming to see my Christmas program, aren't you? I'll be the angel that tells about Mary and the Baby Jesus. I get to sing a lullaby. You want to hear it?"

"Not at the breakfast table, Rebekah dear," her mother protested gently.

"We'll just have to wait and see," her father answered. "If I must miss, it will be for the sake of the Cause."

"For the sake of the Cause!" David erupted. "That's all I hear—for the sake of the Cause! Everything I want to do that's any fun, I can't do it—for the sake of the Cause—just because I'm the preacher's kid."

"David, we don't talk that way at the table," the pastor gave his son a stern warning.

The boy pushed back his chair, stalked to the door, then turned and let loose a torrent of stored-up resentment. "I'll be so glad to finish school this year and go someplace where I can be myself for just once. Everybody in my class got to see the moving picture they brought to school last month— everybody but David—and why? It was wrong for the preacher's boy to see it—for the sake of the Cause! All my friends can play Hearts and Pinochle, but I can't even bring baseball cards into my house. The preacher's kids have to give up cards—for the sake of the Cause! Everybody else turned out for the town square dance to raise money for the new fire station after the old one burned down, but could I go? No, the preacher's kid has to give up square dancing—for the sake of the Cause! And now you'll probably be away again for Christmas this year at some dumb old meeting—for the sake of the Cause! Go on! See if I care!" He turned and was gone, giving the door an angry kick behind him.

"Well! What brought that on?" Sam asked with a pained expression.

Sarah Ogletree turned to the younger members of their tribe. "You've finished your breakfast, children. You may be excused. I'll clear the table for you." Obvious relief at being excused from their chores called for a quick exit before Sarah changed her mind, and the three youngest Ogletrees scurried from the room to other pursuits.

Sam coughed nervously and excused himself as well, but it was too late.

"Not so fast, Brother Ogletree!"

Sam felt the sarcasm in her voice. "Yes, Sarah? Do you have further business with me?"

"Don't be coy, Sam. You have answers for all your flock, but you don't know the hurts of your own boy. It's his last year at home. He's given up some fairly innocent pleasures to protect the good name of his father in this hypocritical little town. Christmas is the one time our family used to be together and enjoy one another. David wanted it to be so perfect this year; and here you announced yesterday that you'll be gone at Christmas because of some great soul-saving crusade in Amarillo. To David, it's one more time that he loses something important to him—for the sake of the Cause!"

"But nobody ever said anything before. Why so much anger now?"

"Me? I'm just jealous of that frilly woman evangelist. For David, it's stealing away the last chance for something special to him. Things are never the same, once a person leaves home. He had it all figured out in his mind that this last Christmas would be a time he could look back on and draw strength from. He wanted it to be just our family, all of us together, loving one another and laughing together at Christmastime. He couldn't handle the thought of your being away—not even for the sake of the Cause."

"You're a better woman than I deserve, Sarah." He bent to brush aside a tear. "Don't fret yourself another minute. I've been a pompous fool. Aimee has so many preachers fawning over her that no one will miss my appearance at her 'grand crusade.' I'll be here for Christmas."

He walked toward the door, then turned and said curiously, "I didn't know David felt so strongly about the things I've expected from him. The Cause of Christ has been my whole life. Have you resented any sacrifices I've asked of you?"

"Of course not, Sam. I fell hopelessly in love with that boyish grin of yours a long time ago, and I've loved you for better or for worse. And I love Jesus, too, Sam, but I think you've made it a little hard on the children sometimes."

"But Sarah, we can't take his Cause lightly."

"Sam, David and all the children love you, and they don't want to embarrass you with their conduct. They believe in the Cause, too, but it seems, even to me, that ever so often the Cause gets confused with some pretty trivial things."

"What do you mean, Sarah?"

"Well, the Sunday you stood up in a brand-new silk suit and a gold stick pin and exhorted on 'the vanity of young women who wear those mannish-looking middy blouses just to be stylish'—that wasn't one of your finest hours. And I seem to remember in that wonderful story Jesus told about a father's love, the prodigal came home to a veal barbecue and a dance."

Then Sarah did one of those instinctive little things a woman has a way of doing—she walked over and kissed him. "I love you, Sam."

The poor flustered preacher was too stunned by it all to know what to say. He cleared his throat, smiled weakly, and bolted out the door.

The next few weeks were filled with the bustle of baking, wrapping presents, doing errands, and putting special holiday touches about the house. David had secured an afternoon job as janitor at the jail to save money for Christmas, so it fell to young Matthew this year to go with his father in search of a tree. The rolling Panhandle plains had little to offer. The few junipers that grew in the canyons were too far away to reach by wagon; and besides, not many ranchers were excited by the idea of folks cutting down any kind of tree that could withstand the wind and sandstorms of West Texas. So father and son settled for three well-formed tumbleweeds, each successively smaller than the other. The Reverend Ogletree found a sturdy rod and wired the wind-dried shrubs to it in such a way that he was able to produce, to the delight of his waiting female critics, an amazingly graceful Christmas tree. The children added strands of red chili pods and popcorn, green rope, and ornaments saved through the years, along with the childish creations from Sunday school craft sessions, until the tumbleweed tree gave the house as warm a feeling of Yuletide celebration as any spruce or pine.

On the Sunday night before Christmas, the Ogletrees marched to their seats to enjoy the Nativity pageant. Brother Sam dutifully gave the opening prayer. He prayed for the sick and the well, for the widows and the orphaned, for the lonely and the homebound, for the rich and the poor, for the old and the young, for the President and the Congress, for all the starving children of the world, and only heaven knows how many more he would have prayed for—but the shepherds were shoving one another off the stage; and Joseph became so irritated at the skinny wise man for teasing him about his girlfriend that he hit him in the nose; and the borrowed sheep had messed up the floor and caused the angels to start giggling, with their haloes awry—so Mrs. Ogletree gave three quick tugs at her husband's coattail, and he closed with an abrupt Amen.

The pageant began, and Brother Sam beamed at Rebekah, who made a beautiful little angel, although one of her wings kept knocking the crown off the head of the fat king, who was having trouble enough holding up the pillow stuffed under his robe. She also forgot some of the words, so it developed that the Baby Jesus was wrapped in "gobs of clothes," and she couldn't quite reach the highest notes of "Glory to God in the Highest." But when it was all over, the Reverend Ogletree picked her up, gave her a special hug, and said she was the very best angel he had ever seen. And all the other Ogletrees chimed in, "Amen."

The day before Christmas began with delighted shrieks from Rachel and Rebekah as Brother Sam pulled open their bedroom curtains and called them to the window. Giant flakes of snow were settling on the rooftop and the mesquite limbs, and it was beginning to stick to the ground. Since school was out, the sheriff had asked David to work all day at the jail, so Sam Ogletree called on Matthew and Rachel to help him fill the coal bin in the parlor, so they wouldn't have to wade through the snow on Christmas morning. They helped him feed the horse and do the chores, with an exuberance that suggested their hope that it was still not too late to make a good impression on St. Nicholas.

When the work was finished, father Ogletree gave in to their gentle persuasion and began to roll the fresh fallen snow into a cheerful snowman, with chunks of coal for eyes and a carrot nose and a happy-faced smile created with red chili pods. When Sarah sent Rebekah out with a discarded hat and an old cane, their handiwork was complete. Rachel ran to her father and hugged his waist. "Oh, Papa, this is the best Christmas we've ever had."

Sam Ogletree smiled too. "Yes it is, Rachel. The best we've ever had, and it hasn't even come yet."

The Christmas Eve dinner always tempted Sarah Ogletree to find some way to outdo the meal of the year before, and this night was no exception. The children sat on the floor at the foot of the Christmas tree, trying to guess the contents of each package, while the kitchen smells were making them more hungry by the minute. Sam refereed their shaking of presents to see that no one ventured beyond the limits of propriety in discovering the contents, but he too was overwhelmed by the captivating aroma from the kitchen. David was already an hour late. Sam could tell that Sarah was becoming anxious; she was not very happy with the idea of her boy working at the jail anyhow. He recalled tales of some of the rough characters that David had told them after the younger children were in bed, and he knew those memories did little to comfort Sarah now.

She turned to him. "Sam, don't you think you'd better go see if anything's happened? It's not like David to be late."

He tried to cover his own growing fears. "Give him another five minutes. If he's not here, I'll go find him." But he was already moving toward the closet.

Sam slipped on his boots and pulled a heavy mackinaw over his shoulders. He returned to the kitchen to reassure his wife.

"Don't you worry, Sarah. I'm sure the boy's all right, but I'll run downtown and see what's kept him tied up." Sam wasn't sure that was the best way to say what he meant, but he left it at that and turned toward the door.

Just then they both heard the heavy sound of boots being scraped on the side porch, and David burst into the room, brushing snow from his arms. Father, mother, and all the younger children rushed to greet him. With one voice, all seemed to chorus, "David, what took you so long?"

He hesitated, then blurted out, "I brought somebody to spend Christmas with us."

"You what?" Sarah gasped.

"The sheriff decided to send all the prisoners home for Christmas; only there were these two migrants he arrested on Mr. Mason's farm—Jose and Maria Garcia. He was holding them for the immigration folks, and they didn't have any home here to be sent to. So I asked them to spend Christmas with us."

Sam looked at the boy in disbelief. "But son, I thought you wanted this to be a special Christmas—just our family together."

"It *will* be special, Papa. I wanted them to come—for the sake of the Cause!"

He reached out and hugged his father in an embrace the two of them never forgot as long as they lived.

The
Humiliation of
Li Huan Liu

It had not been a good morning for Li Huan Liu, Undersecretary of Agriculture for the People's Republic of China. He struggled to get his thoughts back on the report he was putting together for the meeting of the Party leaders, but the embarrassment of the day's events still burned inside him. He wondered if his old rival down the hall could have heard what had happened and would be chuckling in his jacket at the thought of Li's discomfort. Li tried to reconstruct how he had been so caught off guard.

He had planned everything perfectly to impress the Party Chairman with the accomplishments of his region. They had selected a commune with such productivity that even the junior bureaucrats in his unit, always anxious to curry favor with him, had not fathomed the enormity of its achievement. He had taken the chairman with him to the farm, where they had ridden past field after field of the most lush growth they had ever seen. They studied all the figures in the commune office, and it was truly evident that one sector had outstripped even the government's experimental station. They searched for a clue to the secret, but all they could learn from the head of the operation was that one brigade leader somehow could inspire such confidence in his farmers that they achieved what no one else could.

Li invited the chairman to ride with him across the fields to meet young Peng Zhou. They drove through fields with corn so tall it seemed to swallow the car, then waved to industrious men and women who shouted a friendly "Ni hao"* from rippling rows of grain. At the end of the roadway a young man was harvesting pods in the mire of a lotus bog. When Li

*The traditional Chinese greeting of welcome—literally, "You good?" or "How are you?"

asked for the brigade leader, Peng Zhou, the friendly face answered, "I am Peng Zhou."

"Yes," the chairman roared, "I should have known. A man with your record wouldn't back away from sloshing in the mud with his comrades. Can they spare you for a few minutes?"

The man climbed up the bank from the lotus bog and washed the mud from his hands and feet in the irrigation ditch. Then he rolled down his trouser legs and greeted the chairman with appropriate courtesy. "Have you eaten this morning? Will you come to my humble cottage for rice cakes and tea? The grandmother can have it ready quickly."

"We will be honored to sit in your dwelling, Peng Zhou. Show us the way."

The brigade leader climbed into the chauffeured vehicle, wondering whether he should fear or celebrate this sudden attention from men he had thought he would never even get close enough to see; and now they were coming to his own home!

The official car pulled up in front of a small house with an immaculate garden. Bright-blue trim softened the drab gray of the concrete walls. Peng opened the door and called out, "Mama Hwang! We are most honored to welcome guests. Prepare rice cakes, and tea from the tenderest leaves." He offered his guests the hand-wrought chairs in their small living room and took a seat on a stool in the corner.

Since it was evident he had not accomplished what he had done by timidity, he dared to ask, "How have I been counted worthy to entertain such men of stature in my small cottage?"

Li Huan Liu leaned forward in his chair with pride in the young leader. "You have brought credit to the People's Republic of China with your model farm. The chairman wanted to come himself and bring his commendation. Since you became their leader, the workers in your brigade have done what it is not possible for human hands to do, and yet it has been done again and again. Your crops flourish, your houses are spotless, your fields are free of weeds, your harvest is a picture of perfection. What is your secret?"

The family matriarch set cups before the Party officials and poured steaming water over the green tea leaves. When the chairman repeated his question, the woman glanced at the young man as if to reassure him. Peng hesitated, and the ready smile with which he had welcomed the Party leaders wavered.

Li Huan Liu could sense some struggle testing the soul of the younger man. Then the old woman turned and looked into the eyes of the Agriculture Undersecretary. He felt her penetrating gaze, and something seemed familiar in her face. He could tell, too, that she had caught his sense of recognition.

Again the Party Chairman questioned Peng. "Surely you have some way of leading, some technique for production that could increase the yield of all the farms in China. The People's Republic is proud of your generation of pragmatists—smart, creative men who will shape the glory of the Party and of our people. We need more men like you. There could be a place for such skills as yours in the leadership of the Party. Don't be bashful, man. How have you achieved such a record?"

"I have not done it alone. My men and women, even the boys and girls, have brought glory to our brigade. I am only one."

"But you have inspired them to do the task. Such achievements are always the extension of one man—the committed leader. How did you induce their success?"

The young man shrank from answering as if he were a small boy about to try his first dive into a swollen stream. A quick glance at the grandmother's face seemed to reassure him, and he almost whispered, "We are a Christian brigade.

All that we do, we do for Christ, our leader. He gave himself for us and bids us love one another as he has loved us." Peng Zhou gained courage as he spoke. "We plow the fields with joy because we know he works beside us, to help us feed our brothers and sisters in the China that we, too, love."

Silence hung in the air like the stream of smoke from a candle just extinguished. Then the old woman turned to Li and spoke gently. "*You* understand, don't you? Your mother taught you well."

Li's face flushed as he rejected the grandmother's familiarity. "What do you mean, old woman? I never saw you before in all my life!"

"Yes, Li Huan Liu, you have seen me. I was your Sunday school teacher in the little Flower Drum Church. When you were only five years old, you could sing 'Jesus Loves Me' louder than any of the other boys and girls. Surely you remember those happy years—and your mother's religion. You can never forget that."

"It was all very long ago," Li seemed wistful as the memories flooded back. "China has changed since then, and I have changed. The old fairytales about Jesus do not charm me any more."

"How can you say that and remember your mother's devotion, the prayers she taught you at her knee?"

The man's brief tone of gentleness now turned harsh. "When your 'Christian' Chiang Kai Shek turned loose his army on our little village, the greedy soldiers ransacked our home. And when my mother resisted their vulgar advances, one 'brave' man beat her senseless with the butt of his rifle. That is what I remember about my mother. Your God failed her when she needed him most."

"I too have stood in the shadow of grief." The woman looked deep into Li's eyes. "God does not spare any of us the hurt that is common to all humankind. Each of us sooner or later suffers from the sins of another. But God makes us strong, to face life with a good conscience and a faithful heart. Justice comes, though for some it is not fully seen this side of eternity."

"Yes, I was waiting for that—the 'Sweet By and By.' That's why I found my answers in the Communist Party—the power that gives us action now, in the sweet today and today."

"I must take your word for it, Li Huan Liu. But if you ever have some questions the Party cannot answer, you still have an Elder Brother who knows."

The Party Chairman had sat through the conversation as one detached, no emotion showing as he watched Li's consternation at the direction the events of the morning had taken.

"Mr. Chairman," Li turned to his superior stiffly. "What action shall I take toward Peng Zhou for leading the workers astray?"

The Head of State rose from his chair and walked over to Peng Zhou. "You are a gracious host and a fine leader; but your strategy will not work for all of China."

"No, Mr. Chairman, for it is not a technique. It is a way of living—something that must come from the heart. I will step aside so that a new brigade leader can come and do as you wish."

The chairman gave him a faint smile, his first of the day. "No, keep your post. In the new China there is a place even for radicals like you; but you will understand why I can't have a ceremony of recognition for your brigade."

"I understand; and I thank God for your forbearance."

"Thank not God, young man, but your record of achievement. We need your produce too much to give you up. Zai jian."*

*A traditional Chinese phrase that approximates *good-bye.*

The Agriculture Undersecretary followed the chairman to the waiting limousine, wondering what scorn his superior would heap upon him. As they drove back through the crop-laden fields he dared to ask, "How shall we speak of this?"

"How shall we speak of what, Comrade Li? I do not remember anything this morning but the beauty of green fields and happy workers in the Party's commune."

"How clumsy of me," Li shivered with relief. "Of course, nothing unusual at all took place. Yet one thing troubles me still, Mr. Chairman. I hope you will not be influenced by the old woman's words. That is a past I had long since forgotten. She recalled memories that are bitter to me."

"Don't think of it, Li. Most of us did things for our mothers that we would shudder for our comrades to know. We will both blot out this morning as if it had never been."

Back at his desk in the office, the Undersecretary of Agriculture could not so easily force from his thoughts the events of the morning. He felt reassured by the chairman's vindication of his Party loyalty. But that didn't explain the success of the Christian brigade and the young leader's attempt to answer their questions. And why, why, why—after all these years—did the grandmother have to enter his life again? The kindly questioning eyes still haunted him. But enough of such distraction!

He pored over the data his assistants had gathered and laboriously put together his report. By late afternoon he had laid it on the desk of the Party Secretary so it could be assembled with the portfolio of achievements from officials in the other departments. Then he slipped away for a breath of fresh air.

A gentle wind was blowing from the river, lifting the smog that hung over the city. It reminded Li of the freshness of the morning as they had walked in the fields of the commune, but that brought to mind Peng Zhou and the memories he wanted to forget. He dodged the shoppers on the bustling sidewalk until he reached the Arts and Crafts Store near the Forbidden City. For months he had carefully put aside his surplus yuans* in a special savings account for this day. He drifted toward the back of the ground floor where the shopkeeper displayed his finest crafts. Li bent over the counter to gaze at the most elegant piece of jade he had ever seen. It was cut with perfect precision in the form of the ancient Chinese symbol for good fortune. He checked the price and counted out the money for the clerk.

As he waited for the storekeeper to package the purchase, Li let his thoughts wander to plans for the evening. A bemused smile touched his lips at the expectation of young Ming Ling's welcome when he called later at her apartment. He had been discreet in his manner as he moved toward a special relationship with his beautiful secretary. There had been misgivings, but he would not be the first top-level official to enjoy the companionship of a pretty young worker in the Party. Already he could see the pleasure on her face and feel her warm embrace when he placed the precious stone about her slender throat. It would be a moment to cherish always.

The clerk handed him the package and Li stepped out into the December night. It was brisk, but inviting as the street lights sparkled along the boulevard. He began the familiar trek toward his home—past the government buildings, along the row of shops, down the little side streets with their cramped dwellings, then onto the parkway where wrecking crews were clearing out the slums to build a new thoroughfare. Beyond the last traffic signal the lane stretched ahead through an open field where the only light came from

*Chinese currency

the starry skies. He looked up into the night and could not miss one shining star, so brilliant it seemed to dwarf all others. He tried to recall his astronomy studies from the college years, but he couldn't remember any conjunction of distant suns that formed in the eastern sky at that point. Perhaps he needed glasses; he had been drowning in paperwork lately. When he looked again the star was still shining, bright as ever. Trying to ignore it, Li watched a shepherd leading a small flock of sheep through the field as he played a haunting Chinese lullaby on a bamboo flute. The bureaucrat winced at the encroachment of the growing city, whose supposed progress would soon eliminate the meadow.

Beyond the field, the reality of city life returned as Li entered the crowded apartment section. Along the street he saw the tragedy of the recent earthquake that had shaken the mountain villages. A pitiful row of refugee families huddled in little lean-to shelters along the walls of the tenement houses and small street shops. He turned the corner quickly to avoid the pathetic sight. As he looked up again into the night sky, it seemed that the star he had seen before was even more brilliant now. Why should that trouble him?

At the end of the block, he discovered the answer. In a lone shelter against a crumbling inn, he saw a refugee woman, her man hovering above her to keep away the night wind. In the woman's arms was an infant. The star seemed to be shining directly above the weary family. Strangely, it seemed he could still hear the bleating of the shepherd's flock on the meadow. Then from years ago, the words came back—We have seen his star in the East. . . . There were shepherds abiding in the field. . . . For unto you is born this day a Savior. "O God," Li cried. "So many things I need to be saved from!"

On an impulse, he bowed before the weary family, lifted the jade treasure from the box in his pocket, and gently placed the chain over the head of the sleeping infant. He muttered an old Chinese blessing, then quickly disappeared into the night.

And along the street, neighbors stopped to hear the voice of a stranger, singing strong and clear, "Jesus loves me, this I know; for the Bible tells me so."

For
Love of a
Horse

The west wind scooped up little swirls of dust from the desert floor and blew them into the face of the Navajo shepherd. He blinked and rubbed the grit from his eyes, wondering why the gods should punish him with this endless drought. He reached for his water pouch, then scowled when he remembered he had poured the last precious drops down the throat of a panting lamb. He shrugged and turned his flock back toward the entrance to Canyon de Chelly.

Suddenly the man stiffened at the rustling of leaves behind a granite boulder. He relaxed as a frail girl clambered over the rocks and ran to greet him. Her dark eyes were dancing as she held out an earthen pitcher of spring water.

"Yáátééh,* my little Didibah. You always know what your father needs." He swept her up in his arms and downed the drink in one grand gesture. The child kept a tight grip on his shoulder as he drove the sheep down the sloping floor of the canyon. Her left arm swung limp at her side.

The shepherd set the girl down at the gate of the corral and went to pen his flock. Life was not easy for Chee Yazzie. His woman was a fragile creature. He could see her graceful arms moving up and down the loom outside their hogan. Of the three children Shima had borne, only this one, a slender girl with a shriveled arm, lived. Other men had strong sons to follow the sheep and plow the fields of corn. But one does not argue with the gods. How he had offended them he was not sure, but he must be patient. Perhaps yet a son would come to him, strong and manly, to share the toils of Navajo life.

He closed the gate of the sheep corral and reached for the hand of Didibah. "How was school this week?"

*Yáátééh—the traditional Navajo greeting.

"It was fun, my Father. I learned to add numbers and subtract them and do times tables."

"So much in one week? You'll have to be my teacher." Chee had given in to the pleading of his woman and girl-child and had let Didibah attend school. It seemed such a waste for a girl, but to his amazement she had been a brilliant student. That was some consolation, but he was troubled by the ideas she brought home. Their best choice had been the white man's school at Chinle, where the child would not have far to go.

Things had gone well at first. They taught her about the Earth Maker, and that was good; but then she started coming home with strange stories about a Jesus God. Chee had stubbornly insisted that she could not go to the school if it turned her from the old ways of their fathers. So the child would be silent about such things, but some nights when she whispered her soft prayers, he seemed to hear the name of the Jesus God.

The fragrance of the evening meal brought him back to the present as they reached the hogan. His woman, who had left the loom for the cooking fire, turned to greet him. She laid a new blanket at his feet. "For Chee Yazzie, I have made an offering to our gods."

He smiled to see the Rainmaker and the little puffs of cloud in the pattern of the rug. "You are a good woman, Shima. Surely the gods cannot resist your labor of love."

Then she set before him a pottery dish of hot fry-bread. Chee broke the bread and dipped a chunk in the mutton stew bubbling over an open fire. He savored the flavor while his woman rubbed his back with soothing oil. He knew only contentment as the soft wind sighed through the squawbush branches on the canyon floor.

He turned to the child. "Come here, Didibah. The old mare is getting heavier every day. Soon she will have a colt. It will be yours. Then your father will not have to take you to the school bus. How about that?"

"O my Father! My Father!" She rushed to him with a warm hug. The man chuckled to see her stand by the door and look toward the mare with large expectant eyes.

Night came quickly to the canyon. Clouds rolled in over the plain, and the gentle breeze grew cold and fierce. The first spattering raindrops fell before the woman could dismantle her loom; then the skies opened and poured torrents of water down the canyon walls.

"That is their way!" Chee cried out. "The gods of storm arrive with the same vengeance as the gods of drought. Mark my words—the mare will foal tonight. And the gods will laugh!"

The whinny of the mare fulfilled his prophecy in the darkest hour of the night. When morning broke Chee Yazzie led Didibah to the stable for her first glimpse of the new-born foal. In the weeks that followed he watched the girl care for the young colt. She began to do amazing feats with her stump of an arm, things he never had believed she could do—brushing the little animal, weaving her own saddle blanket for the day the colt would be broken, and already training the creature to be clay in her hands.

One morning Chee called the girl. They would go on a rabbit hunt to the upper plain. The colt saw the two hunters coming and trotted toward them. Suddenly he reared—Chee saw a rattler coiled, ready to strike. He lifted his gun and fired, blowing the head off the serpent's body. The colt bolted at the sound of the gun and stumbled over a boulder beside the path. The man froze as he heard the cracking of a bone. He and the girl ran to the wounded animal and knelt beside him. The man felt the fore limb of the colt and found the cracked bone. It was a bad break. The foal would never walk again. Chee looked at his frail daughter and a flood of sympathy surged through him.

"Why do the gods torment me? What can I say to the girl?" he wondered. "Better to be honest." Turning to look into the child's eyes, he groped for the right words.

"Didibah, we can't save him. I'm sorry, little one." He reached for the hunting rifle.

The girl looked at him in horror. "No! No, my Father, you can't!"

"My child, the horse will never walk again."

"Yes, he will!" she pleaded. "I will make a splint for his leg. He is still only a little colt. The weight will not be too much. We can save him."

"You don't understand, Didibah. Even if we could save him, he will always be a cripple. He would not be worth anything to us. It is the kindest thing to do."

"Is that what you thought about me?" The girl's dark eyes flashed. "I'm a cripple, too, my Father." She threw herself on the colt. "If you shoot him, shoot me too. Go ahead! We are both worthless. Get rid of us both, my Father." Her face was bathed with tears and she would not be comforted.

The shepherd knelt beside the sobbing child. "You are worth everything to me, Didibah." He picked her up and held her close, "You are my world, little one. We will do all we can to save your colt."

He set her down and she knelt beside the fallen horse. "You'll be all right, little fellow. I promise," she whispered.

The shepherd only wished he could be so confident. He dragged his tall frame to its full height and turned in resignation back toward the hogan, leaving the girl to soothe the injured colt.

"Rub his back, Didibah, and speak softly to him. We don't

want him to try to get up and make that break any worse. I won't be gone long."

From the floor of the canyon he gathered poles and tied them with leather thongs to form a bed on which to drag the colt back to the corral. He tied the mare to the crude frame and returned to Didibah and the fallen colt. Carefully they pulled the pained animal onto the bed and slowly guided the mare and her load back down the canyon.

Chee Yazzie remembered how an old medicine man, years ago, had tried to save a pet deer with a broken leg. It was worth a try for the sake of Didibah, whose stinging rebuke kept ringing in his ears. He placed the colt in a narrow chute at the mouth of the corral, swung a heavy blanket under the animal's belly, then tied the ends of the blanket to the corral posts until the colt was almost suspended. That way, the three good legs and the makeshift rig could carry the horse's weight.

He turned to Didibah. "Yes, little one, it just might work," he chuckled, admiring his handiwork.

In the days that followed, he watched the girl and the helpless colt. She was like a mother nursing a sick child. Under her care, the animal did seem to be mending—but would he ever be normal again? Chee waited and watched for weeks. The summer winds were turning cooler. The Earth Maker was smiling on them, for soft rains seemed to fall each passing week.

The colt was growing restless now, and Chee Yazzie checked him more often. He was beginning to put weight on the injured limb. Perhaps it was time to see how well the healing had gone. He examined the leg. The bones seemed firm. They had bonded together, although he could feel a thickening where the break had been. He didn't know what that meant. Time would tell.

"My Father," Didibah called to him one morning. "Look! The colt is standing on the foot that broke. He seems restless. Can we let him go?"

"I think your little mustang is ready. Yes, we will turn him loose. Hold your breath. We will see how good a medicine woman you have become."

The young horse bolted from the corral chute and ran like an unchained prisoner up and down the canyon floor. Chee watched quietly—first the colt, then the face of the girl, radiant like the fresh bloom of the cactus blossom opening to the sun. He watched her jump up and down with a joy he could only envy.

"We did it, my Father. We did it! He walks and runs. We saved him!" She ran to the shepherd and he could not resist the joy of her loving and grateful arms.

"Yes, my little flower. We did it," the man answered softly, but he saw what the child would never see.

He returned to the hogan and Shima. "The horse will always be lame, just like the child, forever favoring the left foreleg. She will ride him and never notice the difference, but they will always be late bringing in the lambs and coming back from the spring and returning from the school bus."

And so it was.

Didibah named her horse Blanket, for the rig by which he had been suspended during the long ordeal of healing. There was no need to break the colt. Chee Yazzie watched the girl as she placed the blanket she had woven on the horse's back, and he let her take the risk she had demanded—to be the first to ride her pet. The animal accepted her frail body as if there were nothing on his back, and thereafter, where there was one, Chee could most often find the other.

Sometimes he would watch them slowly and painfully making their way over the rocks of the canyon trail or clip-clopping far behind while everyone else rode ahead at an easy lope, and he wondered what insanity had persuaded him to give in to a child's emotional outbursts. Other men must snicker to think Chee Yazzie had put a crippled child on a crippled nag.

He knew what he would do! He would give the girl the mare's next colt. When she saw the difference between the two, even Didibah would have to admit she should ride the swift horse and let the lame one loose. But he found to his dismay that a woman's way of seeing the obvious is not always a man's way.

The girl said only, "No, I will ride Blanket."

"But little one, the new colt is swift and sure-footed."

"Yes, my Father, but I will ride Blanket. We understand each other." She turned and rode away, and the man knew the matter had been settled. He would have to live with the consequences of his moment of weakness; but he worried about what the girl would do if the lame horse ever stumbled and fell again. He could picture the two weak creatures hurt and alone on the rocky plain.

He turned to his woman. "The girl will not listen to me. I am afraid for her and that clumsy horse."

"Trust them to the Earth Maker, Chee Yazzie," his woman reassured him. "The girl is wiser than her years."

The man nodded. "Yes, you are right," and under his breath he muttered, "The woman is always right." Why did other men talk as if their women were like docile sheep, poor souls who never had a man's wisdom? Did other men boast only beyond the earshot of their women? Or had the Earth Maker given greater wisdom to his woman to compensate for her fragile body? This gentle creature pretended to lean on his strength, but in a storm she was unafraid; and when his stomach churned with anger, she kept her peace; and when the gods conspired against them, and their lambs died in the sudden plague and he shook in rage, she drew him close and gave him comfort.

"Yes, Shima. The girl has made her choice. I will accept it." In the days that followed he had reason to respect that choice. He could not believe the change the horse had made in the spirit of the girl. She insisted on working with her father as if she were a son. He was surprised to see how much she could do with her good hand. And she struggled with the shriveled arm until she could handle the sheep and, to his amazement, worked them with more patience than the clumsy boy he had hired for lambing season the year before. But sometimes when the sun god scorched the earth, the heat was almost too much for her.

"Come here, little flower," he called one morning. "We will fool the god of the blistering sun."

"I think it will be fun to fool the gods," she laughed. "How will we fool them?"

"We will build a sheep shelter. When the sun god burns too hot for us, we can pull the sheep into the shelter and work on them in the shade."

"I think you mean a *people* shelter, my Father," she laughed.

"I think you think too much, Didibah."

"Then I will stop thinking and help you build the shelter. But won't it be too hot inside the shelter?"

"We will build a roof and only two sides, with the roof high in the front facing the south and lower on the back side. The wind can blow through the shelter, but the sun god cannot come inside. Now, any more questions, little doubter?"

"You are a good father to me. No more questions!"

The sun bore down on them, but the two put their hands to the task until, tired and sweating from their labors, they stood back in the shadows of late afternoon to admire their grand creation.

Chee Yazzie turned and saw his woman coming over the hill to judge their handicraft.

"Yááte̊ṓh! Not bad!" she nodded. "Now, how about spring water and honey and fry-bread? Is that reward enough for your labors?"

"Your fry-bread is banquet enough for a chief and his war council." The three sat down and feasted in the shade of the shelter. A breeze slithered through the frame lean-to and the little family breathed the breath of contentment.

"My Father," Didibah looked up at the man. "The friends of the Jesus God call him the Good Shepherd. Because you are a good shepherd, I think I could like the Jesus God."

Chee Yazzie frowned. "Your talk of the Jesus God troubles me, Didibah. Why do you call him a good shepherd?"

"He talks of the Earth Maker as one who goes out to find little lost lambs and bring them safe to the corral. He loves his lost earth-people even more than a good shepherd like you cares for his lost sheep."

"But I have heard rumors about your Jesus God. What happened to him?"

"Bad men nailed him to crossed pieces of wood because he cared for the Earth Maker's lost sheep."

"Aha! Not much good to have a god who gets nailed to crossed pieces of wood. How can a helpless god do Didibah any good?"

"When Jesus God died, Earth Maker made him like Himself; so he comes to help weak ones like Didibah. He is as the wind and the Earth Maker—you cannot see him. But you can feel him living and helping, the way you can feel the wind."

"No more, Didibah," the man protested. "It is too much for me. I keep my own gods—Changing Woman, Coyote,

71

gods in earth and sky—gods I can see. Don't talk to me any more about Jesus God. Silly god, to get himself killed! Promise me, no more talk."

"Yes, my Father," she nodded obediently. But the way his woman listened to the girl's story about the Jesus God troubled Chee Yazzie. And often at mealtime he thought he could see the child's silent lips whispering the name *Jesus*.

It was only upon the intervention of Shima that he let the girl return to school when autumn came. How much he missed her! But he was excited by the swiftness of her learning and the lessons she brought home to him. He was fascinated by her skill with numbers, the way she could write, and the stories about faraway places she told them around the fire at night. All the while, he would counter her stories with the legends his father had passed down to him, so she would not want to turn her back on the old ways.

But he wondered; in the center of the rug she was weaving, she had put a cross sign and clusters of what looked like sheep. Was it only a creative pattern, or was it to remind her of Jesus God, the Good Shepherd who died on crossed beams? She had not spoken of it since he had pledged her to silence about the matter, but could she drive the Jesus God from her thoughts? He was too proud to ask, but he had a strange feeling when she would sometimes smile for no reason.

The man knew what he would do! He would let the girl finish this year of school, and that would be enough. Already she knew more than Shima had ever dreamed of knowing. Besides, her mother would need her help. The heart of Chee Yazzie was singing. His woman was with child again, and this time she seemed much stronger. The flush of joy was on her face so often that he knew Earth Maker this time would bring to them a son, healthy and strong. Shima would need Didibah to help with the child.

The autumn weeks went swiftly by. They put aside the late maize in the bin and gathered the pumpkins. The harvest gods had been good to him. Let the storm gods do their worst! His family would be safe and well-supplied in the floor of the canyon.

He looked up at the sky. Already the winter winds had begun to whistle through the boxwood. He walked back to the hogan where Shima was making bread. There would be a special dinner tonight. It was Didibah's last day of school before the holidays. Christmas vacation, they called it. The lame horse would be waiting for her at the crossroads where the big yellow bus stopped. He looked again toward the gathering clouds. No need to worry. The lambskin coat would keep her warm enough.

Chee was weary from the day's work—repairing the corral and penning the flock. He had counted them twice, fearing one had been lost; then he remembered that Didibah had begged for one small lamb to use in a pageant at the school. He winced to think how often she wrapped him around her little finger and got her way against his better judgment.

He pushed open the hogan door and fell exhausted on his pallet beside the fire. Shima moved to his side and softly ran her fingers through his hair until he fell asleep. Then she, too, nodded and lay beside him.

The fire in the center of the hogan had burned to ashes and grown cold when Chee Yazzie was roused by the wind shaking the posts that held their home together. He walked to the door and rushed back to wake his woman.

"Shima," he cried, "while we slept, the north wind has blown in a blizzard, and Didibah still has not returned. I do not know how long we lay there in our weariness, but it was too many hours. The ashes are cold. Night has come and the snow is deep on the floor of the canyon, and still the wind is blowing."

"Surely the bus would not have brought her from the school in a blizzard," she reassured him.

"A blizzard can come on so quickly. What if she started back on that limping horse before the storm came? It's four miles over the plains." He reached for his fur-lined jacket and waded out through the snow. Already the whirling flakes had turned the trees and boulders of the canyon into blurry ghosts. He could imagine what drifts there would be on the plains at the top of the canyon. There was no way Blanket could have found his way home in the blizzard. Once even he, Chee Yazzie, had lost his direction in a storm. A horse could freeze to death in this icy wind. He could picture the poor dumb animal, frozen in his tracks, still waiting at the crossroads for the school bus.

Chee waded through the snow to the shed and put a bridle on the mare. With halting steps, she made her way across the canyon floor and labored up the ascent to the plain. At the top of the cliff the snow was blowing with such force the shepherd could not bear to face into it. He could not see beyond his eyes, even the length of a hogan.

"O God," he cried, "whatever gods there be, spare the child. Even Didibah's Jesus God, if you are a god, let her still be safe on the big yellow bus. Take care of her tonight when little lost ones cannot find their way."

He turned and barely made out the trail down the canyon to the hogan. Shima had rekindled the fire when he came shivering through the door.

"She must be on the bus or still at school. No creature can be alive in this blizzard. May the gods pity that poor dumb horse of hers."

The woman brewed a pot of coffee, and for what seemed an eternity, they kept their helpless vigil by the fire. Then as suddenly as it had begun, the wind died and the world was still. Chee Yazzie went back into a night brightened by the full moon emerging from a clearing sky. He rushed to the stall, led the mare out again, and was on his way once more through the drifts toward the top of the canyon. As the horse slowly rose to the level of the plain, Chee searched the horizon. The night was still as death. Everything was white and he could see for miles. Nothing moved. He turned the mare toward the bus stop and scanned the open plain for the horse and the girl, but there was no sign of any creature.

For two weary miles, the mare trudged through the snowy drifts until the man knew it was a waste of effort to move on. No living thing could have survived the bitterness of the blizzard. Then he saw the shelter they had built that summer. It looked so out of place tonight—the two-sided structure no shelter from a storm. He turned toward the lean-to and looked again.

"Oh, no!" he cried. "She wouldn't have stopped at the sheep shelter. Oh, no!"

He goaded the mare to move faster and jumped from her back beside the shelter. The horse—that lame, dumb horse—had lain down against the smaller north opening of the shelter, where his hulking frame and the drifting snows had cut off the biting wind. And there, huddled against his underbelly and clutching the lamb close to her, lay Didibah. The desolate man fell to his knees on the frozen ground and lifted the small girl in his arms. He held her close against his grief-wracked body, with only the stars to look down on him in pity.

Then to his sheer amazement, the child stirred and wakened. She cried out, "O, my Father, you did come!"

Tears touched the shepherd's face as he took it all in. He looked into the glassy eyes of the snow-covered animal and pondered the meaning of this night. Then he whispered,

"Earth Maker became a horse tonight to save little Didibah. Could He not have become a man to save all his earth-people?"

Chee Yazzie lifted the child and the lamb to the back of the mare and rode with them toward the hogan. And the heart of the shepherd rejoiced as the child began to tell him the fascinating story of a Baby born in a manger.